This
PJ BOOK
belongs to

PJ Library®

JEWISH BEDTIME STORIES and SONGS

ACROSS THE ALLEY

RICHARD MICHELSON

ILLUSTRATED BY

E. B. LEWIS

G. P. PUTNAM'S SONS

G. P. PUTNAM'S SONS A division of Penguin Young Readers Group. Published by The Penguin Group. Penguin Group (USA) Inc., 375 Hudson Street, New York, NY 10014, U.S.A. Penguin Group (Canada), 90 Eglinton Avenue East, Suite 700, Toronto, Ontario, Canada M4P 2Y3 (a division of Pearson Penguin Canada Inc.).Penguin Books Ltd, 80 Strand, London WC2R 0RL, England. Penguin Ireland, 25 St. Stephen's Green, Dublin 2, Ireland (a division of Penguin Books Ltd.). Penguin Group (Australia), 250 Camberwell Road, Camberwell, Victoria 3124, Australia (a division of Pearson Australia Group Pty Ltd). Penguin Books India Pvt Ltd, 11 Community Centre, Panchsheel Park, New Delhi - 110 017, India. Penguin Group (NZ), Cnr Airborne and Rosedale Roads, Albany, Auckland 1310, New Zealand (a division of Pearson New Zealand Ltd). Penguin Books (South Africa) (Pty) Ltd, 24 Sturdee Avenue, Rosebank, Johannesburg 2196, South Africa. Penguin Books Ltd, Registered Offices: 80 Strand, London WC2R 0RL, England.

Manufactured in China by South China Printing Co. Ltd. Design by Cecilia Yung and Gina DiMassi. Text set in Meridien Medium. Library of Congress Cataloging-in-Publication Data   Michelson, Richard. Across the alley / Richard Michelson ; illustrated by E. B. Lewis.   p. cm.   Summary: Jewish Abe's grandfather wants him to be a violinist while African-American Willie's father plans for him to be a great baseball pitcher, but it turns out that the two boys are more talented when they switch hobbies. [1. Friendship—Fiction. 2. Baseball—Fiction. 3. Violin—Fiction. 4. Jews—Fiction. 5. African Americans—Fiction. 6. United States—History—20th century—Fiction.] I. Lewis, Earl B., ill. II. Title. PZ7.M581915Acr 2006
[E]—dc22   2005032656 ISBN 0-399-23970-7
Special Markets ISBN 978-0-399-25402-4

Every night, after Grandpa turns out the light, I count to twenty before I tiptoe out of bed and tug open my shade.

Across the alley, I know Willie's doing the same.

During the day we don't play together, but at night, when nobody's watching, Willie and I are best friends.

Last winter, I watched his finger spell out HI through the frost on his bedroom window.

He wrote each letter backwards, and then waved.

I heard the ice cracking as I jimmied open my pane.

"My daddy was a starter in the Negro Leagues," Willie told me, "and he says someday I'm going to pitch in the majors."

The next night, Willie showed me how to throw a real big-league slider.

He knew just where I should stretch my fingers across the stitches.

When spring comes, I sit out on the stoop.

Down the street, those other boys are always batting and having fun.

I see a grounder run full steam through Willie's legs like a rat racing for the sewer.

Then a pop-up drops out of Willie's glove.

Now that it's summer, we open our windows wide and play catch. Most days I'm Sandy Koufax and he's Satchel Paige. Some days we switch.

Grandpa says Jewish kids shouldn't waste time
with baseball.

He thinks I should spend every minute practicing
the violin.

"God gave you a brain, Abe," he says. "Let those
Negro boys play ball."

After Grandpa gives me my lesson, I go to my room
to practice.

Willie leans out his window and asks if he can play.

I tell him where to rest his chin on the chin rest and
how much rosin to slide across the hairs of the bow.

All summer long I teach him everything I learned.

Willie's as natural as Satchel on the mound.

His fingers fly up and down the fingerboard like
the pavement's too hot to set your bare feet on
the ground.

"You'll be the next Jascha Heifetz," Grandpa says proudly one night when he comes to turn out the light.

"I think you're ready for the recital at the temple next Tuesday afternoon."

My palms turn sweaty like I've been caught throwing a spitball.

I want to tell him it was Willie, but I can't think of anything to say.

"Grandpa was a great violinist in the old country," I tell Willie late that night.

"But there was a war and Grandpa was imprisoned and made to work like a slave."

Willie's real quiet now and I wonder if I said something wrong. Maybe he doesn't know about World War II.

"My great-granddaddy was a slave too," Willie finally says. "I never knew any white folk that were."

Then we're both real quiet until Willie decides that it's time we went to bed.

All weekend I stay in my room, practicing.

Willie tells his daddy he's sick so he can stay in his room too.

I know Willie should be working on his windup.

Tuesday his daddy coaches baseball and Willie's penciled in to do the pitching.

I take a break to practice my own windup, so I pass my violin out the window to Willie.

Soon my arm's spinning like the
Coney Island Ferris wheel and his bow's
kicking up so much breeze, there's not
a single fly left to swat in the city.
We're both working so hard,
I don't even hear Grandpa
open my door.

First Grandpa looks at me and then at Willie, and then
he turns back toward me one more time.

I'm holding my breath real tight.

"You'll be the next Jascha Heifetz," Grandpa finally says.
And then he shows Willie the correct position of his bow.

It's Tuesday afternoon and we're walking side by side, like best friends, and everybody's watching.

"Let people stare," Willie's daddy says as he steps ahead of Grandpa and into the temple.

"Ignorance comes in as many colors as talent."

When Willie and his daddy sit down, most people get up and slide across the aisle.

That opens up seats in front for Grandpa and me.

Willie's first notes sound like the radio when I'm searching for the signal that announces the Dodger games.

But then Willie closes his eyes, and you can tell by his face that he's found the right station.

When Willie sits back down, the clapping is so loud, you'd think he'd just walloped a homer.

I tell Willie he sounded great, but he's already rushing me toward the door.

In half an hour Willie's daddy is leading us to the sandlot and I'm penciled in to do the pitching.

I'm standing still, but my stomach feels like it's stuck riding the roller coaster.

My first pitch flies over the batter's head.

I stare down at my feet, but out of the corner of one eye I see Grandpa standing between Willie and Willie's daddy.

They're all cheering me on.

I stretch my fingers,
just so, across the stitches
and I spin my arm like the
Coney Island Ferris wheel.
    My next pitch slides straight
over home plate.